The Lion and th...

Retold by Michèle Dufresne

Illustrations by Max Stasiuk

PIONEER VALLEY EDUCATIONAL PRESS, INC.

One day, a mouse
was walking in the forest.
He saw a sleeping lion

"Look at the lion.
He is asleep,"
said the little mouse.

The little mouse
climbed up
onto the lion's back.
He jumped up and down.

The lion woke up.
"Oh, good! A little mouse!
I am going to eat you,"
said the lion.

"Oh, please don't eat me,"
said the little mouse.
"Please let me go!
I can be your friend.
Maybe some day
I can help you."

6

"Ha! Ha!" said the lion.
"A little mouse like you
can't help a big lion
like me!"

"Please let me go,"
said the little mouse.

"All right," said the lion.

One day, the lion
was trapped in a net.
"Help," cried the lion.
"Help! Help!

"I will not help you,"
said the monkey.

"I will not help you,"
said the snake.

"I am your friend,"
said the little mouse.
"I will help you."

He chewed and chewed
and made a hole
in the net.

12

"You see,"
said the little mouse.
"A little mouse
can help you!"

Even the biggest can use the help of the smallest.

16